Stoicism

Complete Guide to Stoicism

How to Apply Stoicism in Everyday Life, Gain Confidence, Resilience, and Wisdom with the Stoicism Philosophy

Zeno Marcus

Your Free Gift

As a way of thanking you for the purchase, I'd like to offer you a complimentary gift:

- **5 Pillar Life Transformation Checklist:** This short book is about life transformation, presented in bit size pieces for easy implementation. I believe that without such a checklist, you are likely to have a hard time implementing anything in this book and any other thing you set out to do religiously and sticking to it for the long haul. It doesn't matter whether your goals relate to weight loss, relationships, personal finance, investing, personal development, improving communication in your family, your overall health, finances, improving your sex life, resolving issues in your relationship, fighting PMS successfully, investing, running a successful business, traveling etc. With a checklist like this one, you can bet that anything you do will seem a lot easier to implement until the end. Therefore, even if you don't continue reading this book, at least read the one thing that will help you in every other aspect of your life. Grab your copy now by clicking/tapping here or simply enter http://bit.ly/2fantonfreebie into your browser. Your life will never be the same again (if you implement what's in this book), I promise.

PS: I'd like your feedback. If you are happy with this book, please leave a review on Amazon.

Introduction

Whenever two or more people are discussing issues of personal wellbeing, happiness, contentment, character, success, grit, confidence, wisdom, and resiliency, the conversation will inadvertently lead to stoicism, an old philosophy that can significantly change how you live your life.

When you adopt stoicism and make its philosophy, principles, and practice an integral part of your daily life, in addition to improving your overall wellbeing and happiness, you will also develop an enviable character, become wiser, confident, and more successful in every area of your life including relationship and business.

If this assertion seems 'too promising,' consider this. Most successful people such as Warren Buffet, Bill Gates, Jeff Bezos, Elon Musk, Tim Ferriss, Theodore Roosevelt, Bill Clinton, Thomas Jefferson, Ralph Waldo Emerson, Arnold Schwarzenegger, J.K Rowling, and many, many other wildly successful and famous individuals practice elements of stoicism.

The assertion here is not that becoming a stoic or adopting its practices will automatically lead to success, no. The assertion is that by internalizing stoic principles and applying stoic philosophies into your life, your character will change for the better and out of this change, your life will take on new meaning.

What exactly is stoicism though? What are its teachings, core principles, and philosophies? Given that the ancientness nature of stoicism, does its practices fit into our modern day environment and how best can you implement these practices to enhance your overall wellbeing, your life, and the life of those you hold dear?

The purpose of this guide is to introduce you to stoicism and its practice, and above that, to show you how to apply stoic principles into your everyday life and by so doing, become happier, more confident, resilient, wise, and successful in all areas of your life.

To get the ball rolling, we shall decipher the true intent behind stoicism as a philosophical approach towards life.

Table of Contents

Part 1: Introduction to Stoicism

Chapter 1: Stoicism for Beginners

What is stoicism?

From an etymological perspective, the term "stoic," which is from where we derive stoicism, the element of being a practicing stoic, is a derivation of the Greek word stōïkos, a term that means "of the stoa," meaning portico or porch.

In ancient Athens, a stoa or Stoa Poikilê or painted stoa was "a painted porch," a place where the early stoics met to teach their philosophy and to engage the Cynics and Epicureans in debates.

Dictionary.com defines stoicism (the noun) as *"the ability to endure hardships or pain without complaining or displaying feelings."* As we will later discuss, living in unison with nature, which often translates into forbearing pain and hardships, is the principle of stoic teaching.

The consensus is that stoicism, founded in Athens around 301BC by Zeno of Citium, was a school of ancient Hellenistic philosophy. The Hellenistic age, period, or philosophy started with Aristotle, a philosopher during Greece's classical period, and ended at the start of Neoplatonism, the practice of philosophy based on Plato's teachings.

Originally, ancient stoicism went by Zenosism—named after Zeno the founder—and only came to adopt that name (stoicism) because its practitioners would meet for debates and teaching in painted porch or Stoa Poikilê, a public space that allowed anyone to listen to and participate in debates.

The stoic philosophy is about personal ethics that draw from how stoics use logic and view physics—the natural world—and human nature. The philosophy teaches that we are social beings and because of this innate human nature, our happiness can only come from accepting the present moment as is. It asserts that human unhappiness comes from our obsession with the desire for pleasure and the fear of pain or the need to avoid it.

> THE END MAY BE DEFINED AS LIFE IN ACCORDANCE WITH NATURE OR, IN OTHER WORDS, IN ACCORDANCE WITH OUR OWN HUMAN NATURE AS WELL AS THAT OF THE UNIVERSE.
>
> - ZENO OF CITIUM -

Although stoicism has a few basic tenets or key pillars that we will discuss at length later, the main teaching is that we have control over but one thing: our minds and therefore ourselves. Because of this, a good life comes about when we use our mind to understand how nature or the cosmos works, and then align the nature of our lives with nature's intents: fair and just treatment for all, and working harmoniously together.

Ancient (and even modern) stoic philosophy is more about thought control, the ability to control your thoughts, emotion, perceptions, and actions in a world that has become highly unpredictable. Stoicism teaches that we have no control over external circumstances; we only have control over our internal circumstances, our thoughts, actions, and behaviors. Thinking otherwise and expecting our external environment to be complementary to our wellbeing is a recipe for unhappiness.

At the heart of stoicism is one basic teaching: *"virtue is the only good thing"* that all human beings should aim to cultivate. From this basic principle, stoics assert that all other things are external. For instance, wealth, pleasure, and health are external and because of this nature, they are neither good nor bad, their value is as *"material for virtue to act upon."*

Stoic philosophy also asserts that highly charged and destructive emotions result from judgment errors, of which we should seek to avoid. The philosophy teaches that we should aim to practice *prohairesis*, a will that is in accordance with nature. From this teaching, stoicism believes that the best way to determine one's personal philosophy is to look at how a person behaves rather than what he says. It asserts that since "everything is rooted in nature," a good life naturally comes to those who obey and live by the natural order.

Most famous stoics including Epictetus and Seneca believed that "happiness comes from virtue." They taught that stoicism (the practice of) is to enhance one's emotional resiliency to the elements of nature such as misfortune, to practice stoic calm, to become a sage, someone truly free of all that is vicious and morally corrupt. To quote Aristotle:

"...the function of man is to live a certain kind of life, and this activity implies a rational principle, and the function of a good man is the good and noble performance of these, and if any action is well performed it is performed in accord with the appropriate excellence. If this is the case, then happiness turns out to be an activity of the soul in accordance with virtue."

Because of its practicality—and perhaps the fact that sage stoics debated in open, public spaces—stoicism flourished and became very popular especially when emperors such as Marcus Aurelius openly embraced it.

As mentioned, the aim of stoicism is to practice virtue as a way of being in tune with nature and from that attunement, develop emotional resiliency and happiness, what the philosophy calls Eudaimonia, a word of Greek origin meaning happiness or human prosperity.

From the onset, practicing stoics and proponents of the philosophy recognized it as a philosophy whose practical implementation in the form of ethics, the study of how to live your life, is necessary in everyday life. The study of ethics then informed the other two topoi or pillars of stoicism, physics and logic, which we will discuss at length later.

The next chapter introduces you to the most important stoics you should know about as you read on:

Chapter 2: Meet the Stoics

If you are new to Stoicism, knowing the key players is very important because their influence and teachings are equally important to your ability to use the Stoic philosophy to improve every aspect of your life.

Before we start doing that, it is worth noting that stoicism does not discriminate, which is why popular ancient Stoics were from diverse cultural backgrounds. Of the famous ancient stoics we know and will discuss, one was an emperor, another a water carrier, another a slave, and yet another a playwright. Others were soldiers, senators, and other independently wealthy. Stoicism, a focus on the internal state: thoughts, beliefs, and actions, is what connects all stoics.

This chapter is a short biographical account of the most important ancient stoics. By understanding these key figures, you will avoid feeling too lost as we discuss the history of stoicism in the next chapter.

1: Zeno of Citium

Bust of Zeno of Citium

Zeno of Citium appears first on our list not because he is the most notable of all the stoics, but because he takes the credit for being the originator of modern day stoicism. His story is also one of the most interesting ones.

He was a merchant who, once as he was travelling between Phoenicia and Peiraeus, a turbulent sea shipwrecked him. He lost his consignment and ended up stranded in Athens where upon wandering into a bookstore, he met Socrates who introduced him to the stoic philosophy and much later, Crates, the Athenian philosopher. Out of the influences of Socrates and Crates, Zeno developed the principles and values that we now call stoicism.

Zeno did not see his shipwrecking as a bad omen. On the contrary, according to Diogenes, he considered the shipwreck the wakeup call he needed to start living a good life. As Diogenes once, Zeno was fond of jokingly saying:

"Now that I've suffered shipwreck, I'm on a good journey..."
"...You've done well, fortune, driving me thus to philosophy."

Zeno of Citium

As he learned more about philosophy and started implementing it in his life, he started teaching it at the Stoa Poilike, with the philosophy at first called Zenoism, which his followers later changed to Stoicism.

The restored Stoa of Attalos in Athens

Although the stoicism Zeno taught at the Stoa Poilike and the one we practice today are different, the underlying principles and teachings remain largely unchanged, only better explained for practical implementation in one's life. Zeno taught the most important stoic philosophy: that happiness or human wellness comes from living in accordance with nature and reason.

Like other philosophers of his time, none of the writings of Zeno of Citium survived. Most of what we know about him and the early stoics that contributed greatly to the development of modern day stoicism—Cleanthes and Chrysippus—is from Diogenes's work, Lives and Opinions of Eminent Philosophers.

2: Cleanthes of Assos

Bust of Cleanthes

Cleanthes succeeded Zeno to become the second leader of the stoic philosophy/movement.

Birthed at Assos, Diogenes notes that Cleanthes arrived in Athens with four Drachma (early coins), and before attending lecturers offered by Zeno, was a boxer known to attend the lectures of Crates the Cynic.

In a new city with no means of income other than boxing, which was seasonal, devoted to the pursuit of wisdom, and the study of philosophy, he became a "professional" water-carrier, which is how he got his nickname, the "Well-Water-Collector", and the income he needed to fuel his pursuit of knowledge and wisdom. The Roman court did not like this. Through summons, the court asked him to explain why he did not work and instead spent his day studying philosophy. He explained himself by working hard during the night. The court, now amazed by his industriousness, offered him money, but at the advice of Zeno, Cleanthes refused the offer.

After Zeno passed on, Cleanthes became the leader of the stoic school, a post he held for 32 years and used to pass on his knowledge. Chrysippus is his most notable student.

"When someone inquired of him what lesson he ought to give his son, Cleanthes in reply quoted words from the Electra: Silence, silence, light be thy step."

Diogenes, The Lives and Opinions of Eminent Philosophers

3: Marcus Aurelius

Bust of Marcus Aurelius

Marcus Aurelius is an influential ancient stoic. Born to a prominent family, he grew upon to become a Roman Emperor. Although little information exists about his childhood life, the existing texts paint a picture of a serious young man who enjoyed hunting, wrestling, and boxing.

How Marcus Aurelius ascended into emperorship is somewhat by chance. Text shows that nearing his death, Hadrian, Emperor of Rome from 117 to 138 CE, named senator Antoninus Pius as his successor with the condition being that to ascend to the throne, Antoninus, then childless, had to adopt Marcus Aurelius. Antoninus Pius was emperor from 138 to 161 CE; upon his death, Marcus ascended to the throne.

Marcus ruled Rome from 161-180 CE. Although many historians and philosophers consider him one of the five good Roman emperors, his reign was far from smooth. During his reign, the Roman Empire fought against the Parthian Empire, barbarians attacking its northern border, and had to deal with a devastating plague and the growing popularity of Christianity.

During his reign, being Emperor of Rome was the most powerful post in the world—much like POTUS—and as such, Marcus wielded immense power. That despite the power he wielded, power that could allow him to fulfil any of his desires and inclinations, Marcus is one of the most impactful of all Roman emperors is proof that when applied well, stoicism can be life changing.

As illustrated in his Daily Meditations, the diary he kept, we see a man clearly guided by wisdom and virtue as he went about fulfilling his empiric duties. Though his private Journal—the Meditations—we see a man who concentrated his life on being more virtuous, honest, humble, wise, self-disciplined, and sage-like and therefore impervious to external elements and temptations.

Most stoic teachings on inner strength, personal ethics, self-actualization, and self-discipline are from Marcus Aurelius teachings as illustrated in his Meditations, a must read book for all Stoic.

4: Lucius Annaeus Seneca

Bust of Seneca

Seneca the Younger, commonly called Seneca, ranks second on the list of prominent and influential of the ancient stoics. Born in the Southern of Spain to Seneca the Elder, a revered Roman writer, Seneca the Younger schooled in Rome and later pursued a career in politics where he managed to rise to the rank of a financial clerk, a regarded position. Coming from a wealthy family, he was independently wealthy—one of the richest in ancient Rome—and a prominent playwright.

Accused of sleeping with the emperor's niece, Claudius, the Roman Emperor from AD 41 to 54, exiled Seneca the Younger—in 41 A.D—to the island of Corsica. From exile, Seneca the Younger penned a letter addressed to his mother in which he tried to console her during his exile. Eight years after Claudius exiled him, his wife, Agrippina, sought permission to have Seneca freed from exile and allowed to become an adviser and tutor of Nero, a future emperor known for his tyranny and notoriety. Coincidentally, in 65

A.D., Nero accused Seneca of plotting against him and ordered his execution.

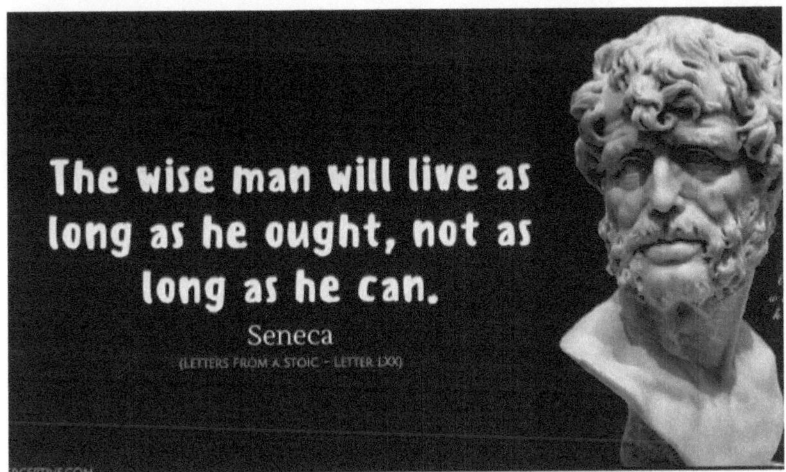

There is no doubt that the life of Seneca the Younger was turbulent—much like our modern lives. Throughout his many troubles in life, Stoic teachings and principles taught to him by Attalus, one of his earliest teachers, gave him the constant strength he needed to persevere.

From his writing, we also know that Seneca the Younger also drew inspiration from Marcus Porcius Cato Uticensis commonly referred to as Cato the Younger.

The most notable of his writing is Letters from a Stoic. The text offers highly actionable philosophical nuggets of wisdom on religion, wealth, handling grief, as well as how to become a man/woman of action.

"Believe me it is better to understand the balance-sheet of one's own life than of the corn trade." "We are not given a short life but we make it short, and we are not ill-supplied but wasteful of it." "Think your way through difficulties: harsh conditions can be softened, restricted ones can be widened, and heavy ones can weigh less on those who know how to bear them."

Seneca the Younger

5: Hecato of Rhodes

> *What progress, you ask, have I made? I have begun to be a friend to myself.*

Although Seneca drew influence from many other stoic philosophers such as Epicurus and Cato the Younger, his writings quote Hecato (or Hecaton) of Rhodes the most.

Hecato was a respected writer who wrote treaties but despite having many treaties to his name, none of his written work survived.

6: Epictetus

Bust of Epictetus

Epictetus is a highly influential ancient stoic. Compared to Marcus Aurelius and Seneca, both of whom were very close to the Roman throne, one as an emperor and the other as an advisor to a future emperor, Epictetus's societal standing is very different.

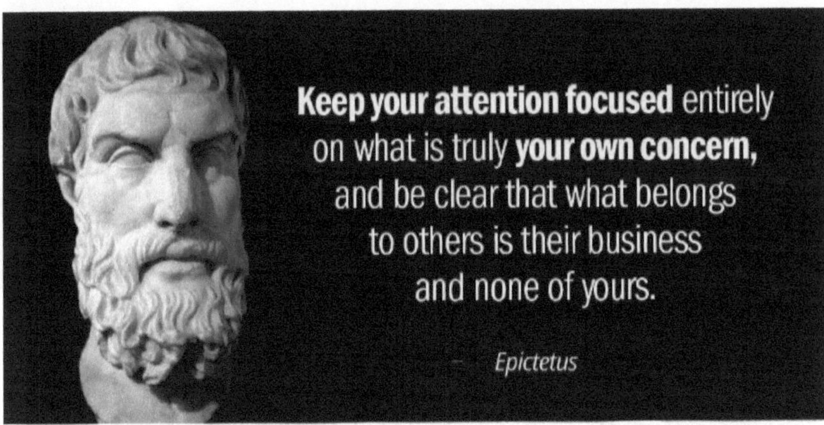

"*Let death and exile, and all other things which appear terrible, be daily before your eyes, but death chiefly; and you will never entertain any abject thought, nor too eagerly covet anything.*"

Epictetus

Born as a slave into the opulent household of Epaphroditus of Hierapolis, Epictetus discovered philosophy when his master gave him permission to study liberal arts; he learned under the tutelage of Musonius Rufus, a revered Stoic of the time.

Shortly after the death of Nero the tyrannical emperor, Epictetus sought his freedom from slavery and after getting it, became a philosophy teacher in Rome where he taught for 20+ years until the Domitian, the Roman Emperor from 81 to 96 A.D. banished all philosophers. He sought refuge in Nicopolis Greece, which is where, after establishing a school, he taught Stoic philosophy until his demise.

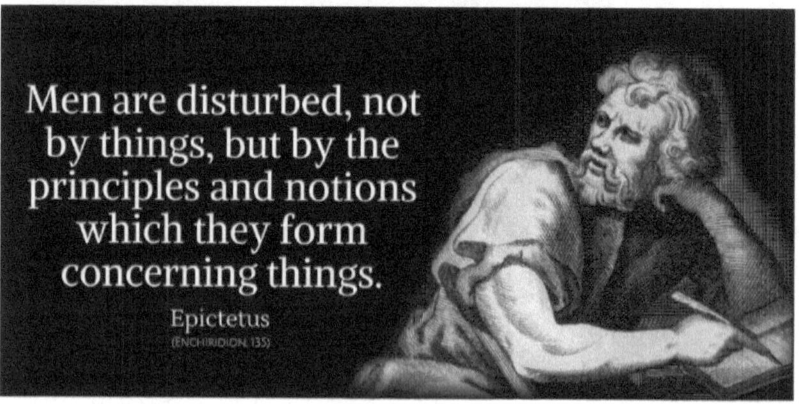

Most notable stoic quotes are from Epictetus. Moreover, his influence permeates the teachings of other equally influential stoic philosophers such as Marcus Aurelius. Unlike other stoics, Epictetus did not write things down. Most of what we know about him and his core teaching come from the notes of Arrian, one of his students. Despite never having written anything himself, his teachings have been influential in the lives of many a great men. Reading his quotes is likely to offer you guidance and be fodder for the self-growth and development you need in your life at any given moment.

7: Gaius Musonius Rufus

Bust of Gaius Musonius

Remembered as a teacher to Epictetus, Gaius Musonius Rufus, the son of Capito, a Roman eques—a knight—, was born in Volsinii, Etruria around 20-30 AD.

Before Nero the tyrannical Roman emperor ascended to the throne, Gaius Rufus was a prominent philosopher and stoic teacher. After ascending to the throne, Nero became obsessed with conspiracy theories and fearing for his life and dethroning him, he accused Musonius of participating in the Pisonian conspiracy and banished him to Gyaruss, a desolate island on the Aegean Sea.

After the death of Nero when Rome was under the leadership of Gaba, Musonius returned to Rome only for

Titus Flavius Vespasianus, the Roman Empire from 69–79 AD to banish all philosophers in 71 AD but Musonius in 75 AD. He returned to Rome after the death of Vespasianus and died there around 101 AD.

Musonius taught practical philosophy: how to use philosophical teachings to live a great life. He taught the principles of living a virtuous and good life as the ultimate path to human happiness and wellbeing.

"...the philosopher does not study virtue just as theoretical knowledge. Rather, Musonius insists that practice is more important than theory, as practice more effectively leads us to action than theory. He held that though everyone is naturally disposed to live without error and has the capacity to be virtuous, someone who has not actually learned the skill of virtuous living cannot be expected to live without error any more than someone who is not a trained doctor, musician, scholar, helmsman, or athlete could be expected to practice those skills without error."

Prof William O. Stephens

Centuries after his demise, Origen, a Greek scholar, noted that Musonius and Socrates were the best examples of how to live the best life.

8: Cato the Younger

Many historians and philosophers consider Cato the Younger someone who lived a stoic life governed by stoic principles and values. Like Epictetus, Cato the Younger did not write any substantive stoic texts. How he chose to live his life and undertake his daily actions, however, was highly influential in the philosophical sense in existence back then.

Born into a well to do family of notable political leaders, Cato the Younger spent most of his life in servitude of the masses; in addition to being a stoic philosopher, he was also a soldier, an aristocrat and a Roman Senator.

As one of the most notable Optimate, a group of traditionalists who sought to preserve the old Roman constitution and system of Governorship, Cato the Younger was a vehement critic of Julius Caesar and his leadership to a point where he would at times act as the leader of the opposition.

Out of his opposition of Julius Caesar and his devotion to his incorruptible morals and support of the Optimates, when Cato the Younger learned that Caesar would triumph at the Battle at Thapsus in 46 B.C. and become Emperor of Rome, he chose to commit suicide.

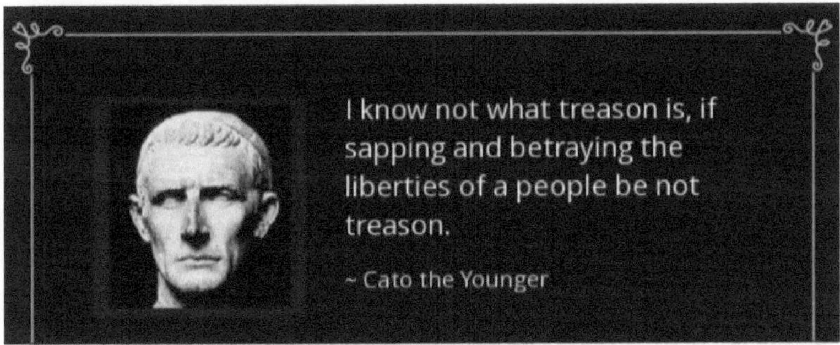

The story of Cato the Younger as told in *Cato: A Tragedy in Five Acts*, a popular play in Ancient Rome—especially how, out of principle, he took his life to avoid living under the rule of Julius Caesar—inspired many a great men of the day who quoted Cato the Younger in their public and private speeches. It also inspired great men of later generations.

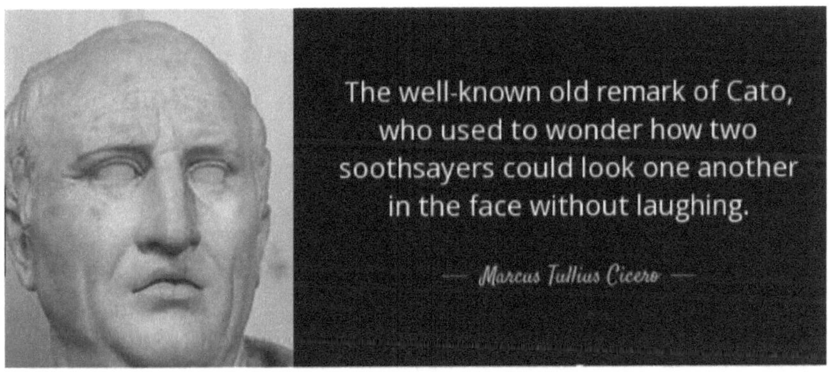

It inspired George Washington and the revolutionary war, Benjamin Franklin who used lines from the play as his motto and the opening lines in his diary, and John and Abigail Adams whose love letters to each other had quotes from Cato the Younger.

Although he was quiet and reserved, Cato the Younger is one of the most stoic of all stoic philosophers of his time, thereafter, and even to date. He was very fond of saying:

"I begin to speak only when I'm certain what I'll say isn't better left unsaid."

Cato the Younger

The life of Cato the Younger is full of lessons that every stoic should adopt, internalize, and practice daily. The Quote above is a great example. We should all aim to speak only when what we have to say is important enough to say. If something is not true, helpful, inspiring, necessary, or kind, we should not say it.

Since its initial establishment, stoicism has developed greatly. The next chapter looks at the rich history of stoicism.

Chapter 3: Brief History of Stoicism

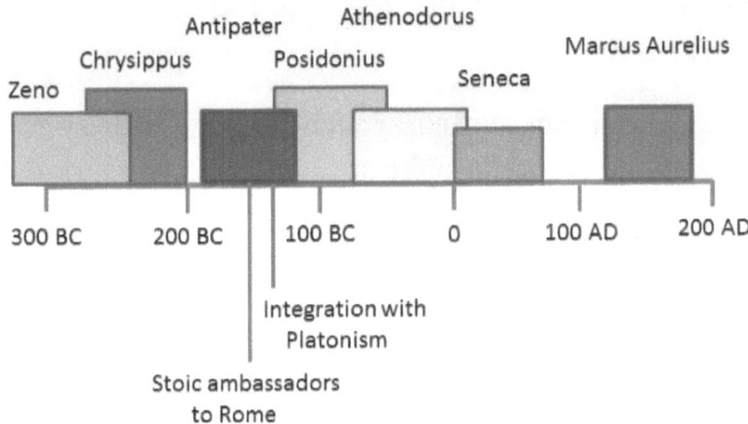

Stoicism has a rich history. Most philosophers and philosophical scholars note that ancient stoicism underwent three major phases. The first phase was the ***early Stoa***, which is from the time of its founding by Zeno of Citium (around 300 B.C.E) to the time of Chrysippus of Soli, the third head of the school.

The second phase, the ***middle Stoa***, encompasses I and late II century, under the leadership of Panaetius of Rhodes, Posidonius of Apameia (or Rhodes), and the Roman Imperial Period.

The third phase, the ***late Stoa***, occurred in I and II century C.E. and is the developmental stage where we find famous stoics such a Marcus Aurelius, Seneca, Epictetus, and Gaius Musonius Rufus.

Early Stoa was the most popular philosophy among the elite of the Roman Empire and the Hellenistic world. Gilbert Murray, a renowned classical scholar noted that most successors of Alexander the Great considered themselves practicing stoics.

Historically, stoicism started around 300 BC with Zeno of Citium teaching the philosophy at the painted porch or Stoa Poikilê, which is how the philosophy adopted the name stoicism—previously called Zenosism.

During its early development under the leadership of Zeno, it is worth noting that stoicism was not the only existing philosophy; other schools of philosophy existed with one such school being the Epicurean school of philosophy, a materialistic philosophy based on the teachings of Epicurus.

Unlike these other schools of philosophy, Zeno and early stoics chose to teach their philosophy publicly at a central gathering overlooking the Agora. They would engage all, including the Epicureans and Cynics in debates about the nature of life. Of the stoics of early stoa, other than Zeno, Chrysippus of Soli was the most influential and the one most credited with modern day stoicism.

Historical Background

The previous chapter mentioned that Stoicism is a Hellenistic, eudaemonic philosophy, the implication of which is that although it was openly critical of them, the philosophy drew greatly from preceding Hellenistic, eudaemonic philosophies. It drew from and openly disagreed with

Socratic thinking, Aristotelianism, skepticism, Epicureanism, cynicism, and preceding Greco-Roman philosophies.

Most of these philosophies used the term "Eudaimonia," a term that has a literal, modern-day translation of happiness or wellbeing in the broadest sense of the word, to mean a life worth living. For most of these philosophies including stoicism, Eudaimonia involved living a morally virtuous life, an idea that drew from the virtue ethics associated with Aristocratic and Nicomachean ethics.

When related to the different scholastic philosophies of the time, stoicism displays some differences. For example, in the Euthydemus, Socrates argued that virtue, importantly, the virtues of temperance, courage, justice, and wisdom, are the most important, in his words, *they are the only good* and that all else is neutral: neither good nor bad.

On his part, Aristotle had a list of twelve important virtues but held that in themselves, virtues were not enough for the attainment of Eudaimonia. Aristotle taught that in addition to being virtuous, experiencing Eudaimonia also needed other elements such as a degree of good looks, wealth, education, and good health. Aristotle held that a good or flourishing life comes from the cultivation of good character, being virtuous, and part luck in the sense of living in accordance with the natural, cultural, and physical conditions that often shape and influence our lives.

In contrast, Cynicism teachings were extreme. Like Socrates, they believed that virtue "was the only good." Unlike Socrates, however, they taught that the external "elements"

Socrates advocated for were mere distractions that deserved conscious avoidance. Most famous Cynics of the time such as Diogenes of Sinope lived eclectic lives.

"[37] One day, observing a child drinking out of his hands, he cast away the cup from his wallet with the words, "A child has beaten me in plainness of living." He also threw away his bowl when in like manner he saw a child who had broken his plate taking up his lentils with the hollow part of a morsel of bread...."

Diogenes of Sinope

Diogenes and the boy without the cup

The first and second phase of Stoicism cover Greek Stoicism, early I century B.C.E. from the period of its establishment by Zeno, to its wide adoption, support by notables such as Posidonius, and rapid growth from Athens to Rome.

Early Stoicism was very "Socratic" in nature: it drew greatly from Socratic teachings. Likewise, stoicism also drew from Cynicism; in fact, Zeno started his studies under Crates of Thebes, a Cynic, and later Stoic writings from the likes of Epictetus drew from Cynicism. Zeno also studied under Polemon of Athens, the head of the Platonist academy of philosophy, and Stilpo, a Megarian philosopher.

These influences are important to understand because Zeno's stoic teachings were Socratic in nature in that they considered virtue as the Chief Good and highly important to Eudaimonia, but also acknowledged that the secondary, external goods advocated for by Polemon and Stilpo had neutral value since they were neither good nor bad.

Many Stoic philosophers credit Zeno with developing the three Topoi or tripartite study that make up the stoic philosophy: ethics, physics, and logic. The Ethics were a milder version of Cynicism; Physics drew from Plato's teachings, and logic drew from formal reasoning and epistemology, the theory of knowledge—stoics approach to knowledge was empiricist-naturalistic.

The stoics that came after Zeno of Citium often interpreted his teachings different and had divergent opinions. For instance, Cleanthes of Assos and Chrysippus of Soli had divergent views about the union of the virtues. Zeno had chosen to talk about each virtue being a kind of wisdom. Cleanthes took a unitary approach to this and taught that all virtues were one: wisdom. On his part, Chrysippus took a pluralistic approach by teaching that each virtue was but a branch of wisdom.

Despite contravening anatomical evidence already in existence during the Hellenistic period, Early Stoics such as Chrysippus vehemently defended Zeno's writings and teachings on the heart being man's seat of intelligence—as opposed to the brain.

The Imperial period takes credit for the decided shift from the physics and logic, the more theoretical aspects of Stoicism, to the ethics, the more practical elements of Stoicism practiced today. Famous Stoics of the time were Seneca, Epictetus, Marcus Aurelius, and Musonius Rufus. Most indirect historical texts on Stoicism are from this era.

Stoicism was still alive and thriving during the Roman era. However, during this time, the Stoics of the time concentrated on refining the fundamental ideas for practical implementation in their personal and social lives–the three topoi or basic tenets of Stoicism that we shall discuss in chapter 4.

Throughout the middle Ages, the Renaissance, and even today, stoicism has greatly influenced Western philosophy. The Renaissance was an especially stoic-friendly time and stoic books such as Seneca's Letters and Enchiridion by Epictetus were rather popular.

Like most philosophies, stoicism has persisted and is today becoming very common a practice thanks in part to the chaotic nature of modern day life and the practicality of its teachings.

Like Hellenistic stoicism, modern day philosophy is also more about the practical application of the value ethics prescribed by stoicism. Modern day stoics use the practical virtues and principles it teaches as a sort of guidance whose daily adherence to can lead to a good life experience.

In terms of its roots, contemporary or modern day has roots in logotherapy—that finding meaning is our greatest aim and driver—by Victor Frankl, and earlier forms of cognitive behavioral therapy (CBT). Even so, it is worth noting that contemporary stoicism is not a therapy; it remains a philosophy.

Contemporary stoics such as John Sellars, Lawrence Becker, and William Irvine have done a great job of differentiating the English word stoic, meaning someone who is rigid or stiff in the sense of going through life with a stiff upper lip, from the philosophical meaning of Stoic or Stoicism.

Hellenistic Stoicism practiced by the likes of Epictetus, Seneca, and Marcus Aurelius focused primarily on dichotomy of control, "of some things being in our control while others are not." Thanks to modern day stoic philosophers such as William Irvine, contemporary stoicism focuses more on trichotomy, "of specific aspects such as our beliefs, judgements, and actions being in our complete control, and other elements such as nature and history being outside our control, while other things are partially in our control."

Internalized goals are a good example of an element we have partial control over.

Consider the example of a race. Because you have influence over it, you have partial control over how the race turns out. At the same time, the race also has elements outside your immediate or partial control, a great example of which is the skill and level of determination to win exhibited by other racers. In this case then, contemporary stoicism teaches that since winning the race is outside your immediate control, such should not be your aim. Instead, your aim should be to control what is within your immediate control: doing your best and throwing your heart over the fence.

In the 21st century, stoicism has grown significantly and its practical principles become more accessible to all thanks to the development of technologies such as the internet and other technologies that allow us to access information at the press of a button.

Even though stoicism has changed greatly, its basic tenets remain unchanged. The following chapters discuss these core tenets and show you how to apply them in your life so that you can become more resilient, confident, wise, happier, and more successful.

Part 2: How to Apply Stoicism in Your Life

Chapter 4: The Basic Tenets of Stoicism (The Three Topoi)

Stoicism has three basic tenets whose practical application of, according to stoic teachings, leads to a life experience that is in tune with nature.

Stoicism offers a unified account of nature. This account consists of the three topoi or basic tenets that are logic (formal), physics (monistic), and ethics (naturalistic). Of these tenets, early stoicism considered ethics more important to human knowledge.

Before we discuss each of the three topoi individually, it is important to mention and point out that although stoics consider ethics important and central to happiness (the experience of), ethics alone is not enough, which is why it needs the support of the other fields of inquiry: logic and physics.

Also worth mentioning and noting is that from the very beginning, the aim of stoicism was to provide a practical philosophy whose practitioners of could apply in their daily lives and in so doing, experience a eudaimonic or happy life, one guided by key virtues.

As stoicism developed through the Roman era, the aim of the philosophy became using the basic tenet of ethics to achieve *apatheia*, equanimity or a state of mind free from the disturbance of the passions that we will discuss later.

The achievement of equanimity through the practice of cardinal virtue (ethics) required the support of the other two tenets: logic, the theory of knowledge as well as how to reason and think about nature and the world in which we live, and physic, metaphysics, natural science, or the study of the world we live in.

Although individual, the three topoi relate in the following sense. Stoics use the analogy of an egg to show the relationship between the three tenets.

In this sense, logic is the outer shell; ethics is the egg white and physics is the York:

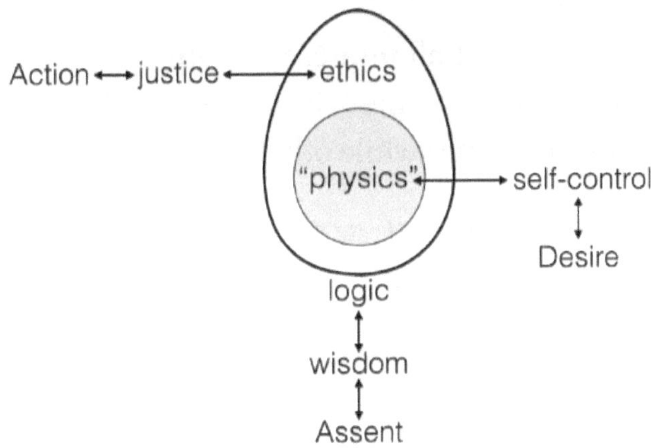

The best way to conceptualize the interconnected of the three topoi is to think of a garden. In this case, logic would be the fence protecting the delicate interior; the nutritive soil would be the physics that enriches your knowledge of the world, while the fruits of the planted plants would be the ethics, the intended aim of the stoic practice.

There is no consensus on the sequential order of implementation of the three basic tenets of stoicism. Most philosophers note that for a naturalistic philosophy such as stoicism is that all the pillars are complimentary and important to the practical implementation of the philosophy in one's life.

1: Logic

Early stoics believed that being a sage, someone who practiced virtue and lived in oneness with nature, meant having good knowledge of the world or things. To cultivate formal logic, stoics relied on (and still do) cognitive and moral progress, an idea dubbed *prokopê*, making progress.

Stoic logic does not hold that all impressions are true; on the contrary, it holds that some impressions lead to comprehension (are cataleptic) while others are not.

> *"The cataleptic, which [the Stoics] hold to be the criterion of matters, is that which comes from something existent and is in accordance with the existent thing itself, and/has been stamped and imprinted. The non-cataleptic either comes from something non-existent, or if from something existent then not in accordance with the existent thing; and it is neither clear, nor distinct."*
>
> Diogenes Laertius

Stoicism also admits that perception is not always right and can be wrong, as is the case with *phantasma*, a term meaning impressions of the mind such as dreams, hallucinations, and other unconscious judgments. The aim of stoic logic is to train, or make gradual progress, towards distinguishing between cataleptic and non-cataleptic impression. Ancient stoics such as Chrysippus maintained that it was important for stoic sages to absorb different forms of impressions as a means to progress.

Stoic logic is about cultivating the ability to distinguish between opinion that is weak or false, apprehension, and knowledge based on firm impression and reason that is beyond alteration or reproach. Stoicism holds that this kind of cataleptic impression is the first step on the ladder to actual knowledge.

Stoic logic is propositional logic, a type of logic concentrated on the validity of arguments rather than the truth per se or logical theorem. The main use of logic in stoicism is to use it to complement ethics and guard against perceptions that may compromise it.

2: Physics

Stoic physics amounts to what we would now refer to as theology, natural science, and metaphysics.

In relation to natural science, the underlying stoic principle is to live "in accordance with nature." This means we should aim to understand nature as best as we can, with its study and comprehension aimed at being complementary to the achievement of a eudaimonic life. Stoicism holds that everything we consider real, i.e. existing, is corporeal but also that some things such as time, void, and sayables are incorporeal.

Ancient stoicism embraced a vitalist understanding of nature governed by two main principles, one active in the form of logos and relating to God and reason, the other passive and relating to matter and substance. The active principle is indestructible while the other took the form of the four elements of fire, water, air, and earth and is therefore destructible to the point of being eternally recurring in nature and the cosmos.

Stoicism notes that the cosmos is alive and guided by a rational principle (logos) called the *aether* or stoic fire, which is different from elemental fire, the fire we know of and that is capable of burning and destroying.

Stoic logic also notes the immanence of God in the universe, a fact displayed by the creative cosmic fire. Unlike Christianity and Aristotelian, stoicism does not believe in a God who is a prime mover or existing outside space and time; they hold that if that were the case, if God was incorporeal, he would be unable to act on things because according to the philosophy, what is incorporeal lacks causal powers.

A core teaching of stoic physic is that all things have a cause. Chrysippus held that it is impossible for motion to occur without a cause. To this, stoicism holds steadfastly to the notion of universal causality as a branch of its physics and explanation of the nature of the cosmos, which is that nature and the future operate within the laws of physics.

> *"[The Stoics] say that it is impossible, when all the circumstances surrounding both the cause and that of which it is a cause are the same, that things should not turn out a certain way on one occasion but that they should turn out that way on some other occasion"*
>
> *Cicero*

Ancient stoics also believed that chance is nothing but human ignorance in the sense that chance happens out of events we humans do not understand.

3: Ethics

Like logos and physics, Stoic ethics are less theory and more practical. Stoic ethics is the study you, a stoic, should live your life. From antiquity, living a life governed by ethics was the aim of the philosophy, a fact that many famous stoics acknowledge as not being easy and therefore requiring *prokopê,* making progress.

"The philosopher's lecture room is a hospital: you ought not to walk out of it in a state of pleasure, but in pain—for you are not in good condition when you arrive!"

Epictetus

The essense of ethics is the acknowledgment that, as the *Enchiridon* notes, we have control over some things and no control over others:

For early stoics, "live in accordance with nature" was the principle motto in ethics. With this, they meant that we should live lives that are in tune with nature (the cosmos), and human nature, to which they noted that humans are social beings capable of rational judgment especially in relation to how to live life.

Close to the idea of following human nature was oikeiôsis, another stoic concept that translates to affinity. Stoicism believes that as humans, we have the natural ability to develop morally and that this natural propensities begin instinctually but are refinable as we age and learn how to reason.

The stoic naturalistic account of how we develop virtues or moral behavior is in line with what we know from cognitive science and evolution. For example, we know that by nature, we always act in a manner that advances our interest and goals be they health or wealth related. We also have the ability to identify with the interests of others, and to find practical ways to navigate through life and its many difficulties.

According to stoicism, these propensities have a direct relation with the four cardinal virtues that govern our lives: courage, practical wisdom, temperance, and justice. To pursue our goals, we need courage and temperance; justice is a natural part of being a human existing in a social society where we have a circle of friends or people we interact with daily. On its part, phronêsis, or practical wisdom, gives us the ability to deal with the many circumstances that make up our lives.

In addition to these four cardinal virtues, stoicism notes that because they relate to each other, each of them has major categories. For example, under practical wisdom are the virtues of good judgment, resourcefulness, and discretion; under temperance are the virtues of propriety, self-control, and honor; under courage are the virtues of confidence, magnanimity, and perseverance. Under justice are the values of sociability, kindness, and piety.

Even with the cardinal virtues as derived from Socrates, the stoic understanding of virtue is unitary—*pluralism*. For instance, justice is practical wisdom applied socially; courage is endurance, and temperance is choice, and as such, all virtues are inseparable—it is impossible to be courageous but not temperate.

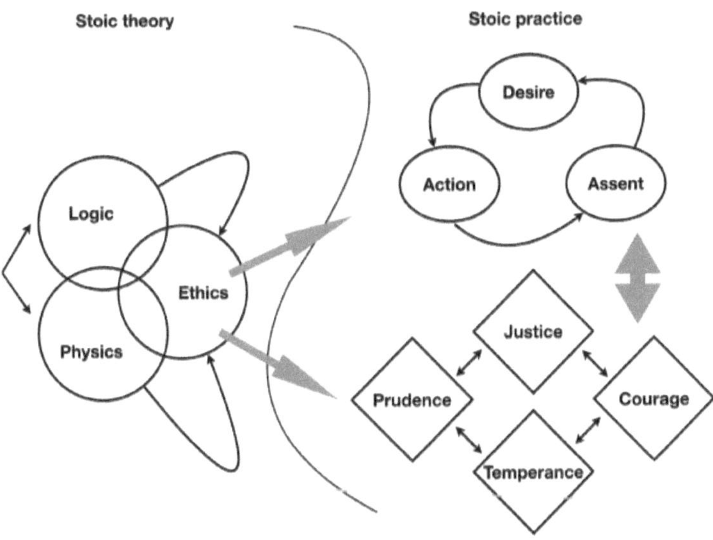

The four cardinal virtues and the three tenets (topoi) that govern stoicism relate greatly to the stoic disciplines of desire, action, and assent that we will discuss in the next chapter and illustrate how to apply in your life in a practical manner.

The aim of stoic ethics is to help you differentiate between the two stoic concepts introduced by Zeno: preferred and dispreferred indifferents.

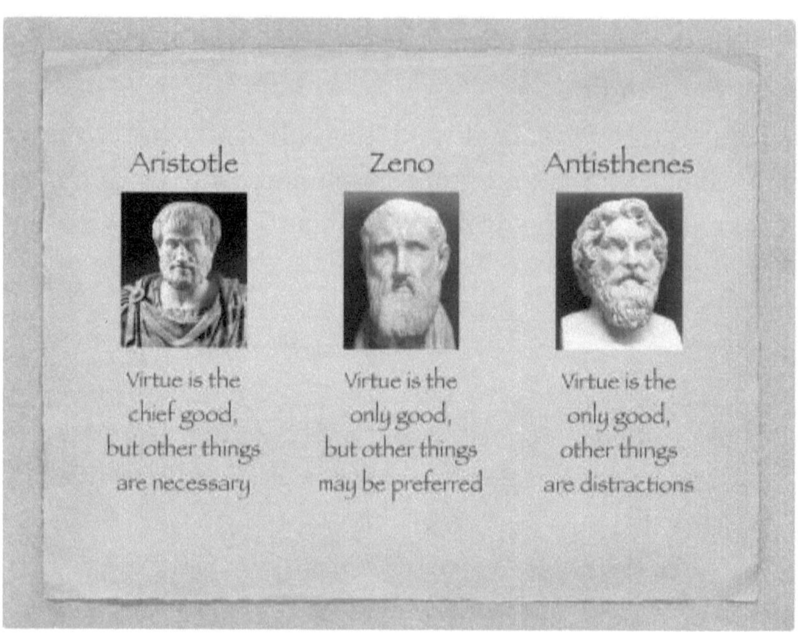

According to Zeno and stoic teachings, some indifferents have value, axia, while others lack it, apaxia. Axia consists of preferred indifferents such as education, wealth, and health. Apaxia consists of dispreferred conditions such as ignorance, sickness, and poverty.

Although stoicism teaches that some indifferents such as wealth, health, and education are preferred, these indifferents are only preferred when they do not compromise but instead enhance the practice of virtue. Even the preferred indifferents are not truly necessary to experiencing a happy or eudemonic existence.

This means that while it is human nature to seek some preferred conditions such as wealth, better health, and education, as long as you practice the cardinal virtues and the ones underneath them, your happiness, wellness, or wellbeing is independent of these external or material circumstances.

From the onset, stoicism held that understanding nature—or if you may, the cosmos—informs our understanding of ethics, the understanding of how to live a eudemonic life.

Now that you have a basic understanding of the three topoi (or basic tenets) of stoicism, let us look at the disciplines underneath or governing each of the tenets.

Chapter 5: Applying The Three Stoic Disciplines

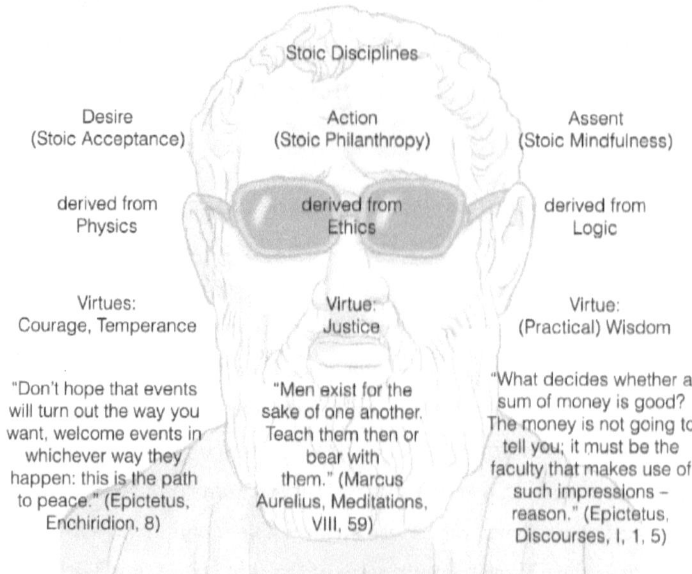

Stoicism is a practical philosophy whose main aim or intention is to help you, its adopter or practitioner, combine the practice of physics, logic, and ethics to help you create a "guide" by which you can base how you live your life and achieve happiness or wellness in every sense of the word.

Thus, early stoics developed the three disciplines of *desire* that primarily concentrates on accepting what is as it is (our fate), *action* that concentrates on love for mankind, and *assent* that has to do with being mindful of our moment-to-moment existence and conclusion/judgments.

Marcus Aurelius, the most popular stoic—at least to modern day stoics—learned these disciplines or principles from Epictetus's Discourses as recorded by Arrian, his disciple, and mentions them several times in his famous writings, *The Meditations.*

This chapter explores the three disciplines and shows you how to implement them in your life in a practical, easy manner:

Worth mentioning is that the aim of the three disciplines—a combination of—is to help you live a life that is in harmony with nature.

Desire: The First Discipline

"The faculty of desire purports to aim at securing what you want...If you fail in your desire, you are unfortunate, if you experience what you would rather avoid you are unhappy...For desire, suspend it completely for now. Because if you desire something outside your control, you are bound to be disappointed; and even things we do control, which under other circumstances would be deserving of our desire, are not yet within our power to attain. Restrict yourself to choice and refusal; and exercise them carefully, within discipline and detachment."

—Epictetus, Enchiridion, 2.1-2

Also called the stoic discipline of acceptance, desire or *orexis*, comes from the stoic topos physics, and concerns itself with the stoic study and practical application of theology, natural philosophy, and cosmology.

Simplified, the discipline of desire is about living a life that is in harmony with nature or the cosmos as a whole—or according to stoicism, a life that is in accordance with God or Zeus, the king of the gods of Mount Olympus.

In practical application, this means being accepting of our fates as an inescapable part of our lives. This discipline especially espouses the virtues of self-control, courage, self-discipline, and endurance especially when facing many of life's difficulties. The aim of this discipline is to help you become aware of, and differentiate rational from irrational, healthy from unhealthy passions and renounce desires that compromise the practice of the cardinal virtues.

The aim of this discipline is to help you be lovingly accepting of your fate, what is outside your control. In the Enchiridion, Epictetus notes this of this discipline:

From this quote, it is easy to surmise that this discipline is primarily about teaching yourself to desire what is in harmony with nature, or rather, what the universe desires for you.

To explain this discipline, the wise Epictetus used the analogy of a dog pulling a cart. Leashed to a cart, a dog can struggle against the movements of the cart thereby ending up miserable and hurt, and decide to go along with his fate and enjoy the ride. The concept Epictetus sought to enforce is similar to what Nietzsche sought to reinforce when he said, "love your fate."

When Epictetus said, "endure," what he meant is that to live a eudemonic life, we must courageously face whatever circumstance life (or fate) throws at us; on "renounce," he meant we should exercise self-control by restraining ourselves from pursuing desires that fail to align with what the universe has in store for us.

Lived physics: How to Apply the Discipline of Desire

When it comes to lived physics, or rather, the practical implementation of the principle of desire, stoicism notes that four passions that further divide into two types that contribute greatly to our misery and hinder our progress. The first one is the desire and fear of things not in our possession in the present moment but that we anticipate in the future. The second is pleasure or distress from what we engage in from moment-to-moment.

The Promise and Warning of Epictetus

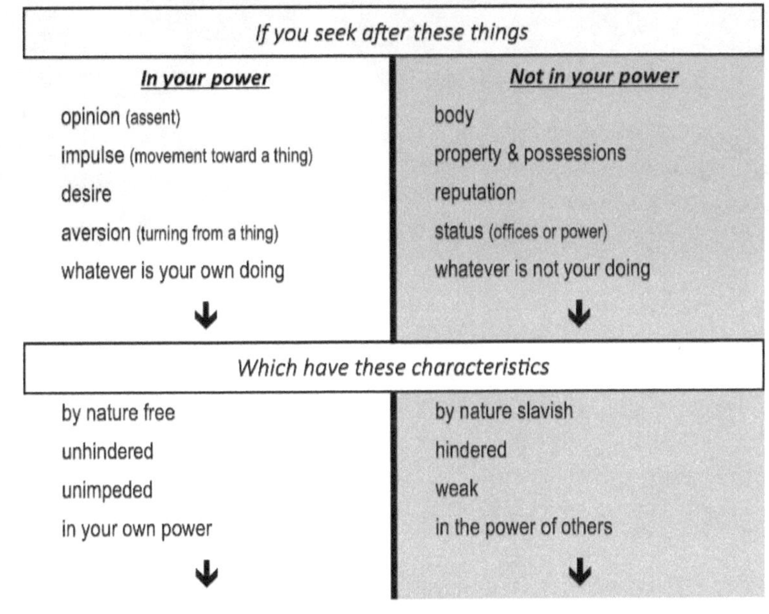

On desire, Epictetus notes:

March 25th
WEALTH AND FREEDOM ARE FREE

"... freedom isn't secured by filling up on your heart's desire but by removing your desire."

—EPICTETUS, *DISCOURSES*, 4.1.175

There are two ways to be wealthy—to get everything you want or to want everything you have. Which is easier right here and right now? The same goes for freedom. If you chafe and fight and struggle for more, you will never be free. If you could find and focus on the pockets of freedom you already have? Well, then you'd be free right here, right now.

If you think about it critically, you will see the sense in this teaching. Rather than sit around desiring for change to happen or wishing that Lady Luck would strike and change your fate, we should take charge of what is in our immediate control; perhaps change our habits, perception, beliefs, and if need be, our social circle.

The discipline of desire teaches us to take responsibility for our actions, ourselves, our happiness, and of course our wellbeing; it teaches that being self-reliant is the key to a eudemonic existence. Essentially, if you have a desire, something you want to get, you have to take 100% ownership of the situation. Leave not your happiness or wellbeing to chance: take charge of the process, control what is in your control and worry not about what is outside your control.

"Nature of any kind thrives on forward progress..." "...And progress for a rational mind means not accepting falsehood or uncertainty in its perceptions, making unselfish actions its only aim, seeking and shunning only the things it has control over."

Marcus Aurelius

To practice the discipline of desire in your daily life, you need to understand two key elements: human nature and acceptance to cosmic nature.

On human nature, stoicism teaches that we should pursue joy instead of pleasure, be rationally cautious instead of irrationally fearful, and wish for, or desire things or circumstances that are in our good and in alignment with the cosmos or nature.

On assenting to cosmic nature, we should learn to trust the rationality and providential nature of the cosmos and out of this practice to desire the best outcome possible. When you attune your mindset and attitude in this manner, you develop the ability to see, face, and accept the good in all events including ones that appear tragic. This helps you develop resiliency to which Epictetus notes:

From everything that happens in the universe it is easy to praise providence, if one has within him two things: the faculty of taking a comprehensive view of the things that happen to each person and a sense of gratitude.

Discourses 1.6.1

Practical application of the stoic discipline of desire calls on you to do more than tolerate or love what happens to you. It calls on you to approach trying circumstances from a cosmic perspective. Not to suck it up but to accept adversity and welcome it with a glad mind; in essence, this means you should *start seeing everything that happens not as happening to you but happening for you.*

Come now, haven't you been endowed with faculties that enable you to bear whatever may come about? Haven't you been endowed with greatness of soul? And with courage? And with endurance? If only I have greatness of soul, what reason is left for me to be worried about anything that may come to pass? What can disconcert or trouble me, or seem in any way distressing? Shall I fail to apply my capacities to the end for which I have received them, but instead groan and lament about things that come about?

Epictetus, *Discourses* 1.6.28-29

Like the dog analogy used earlier, we can choose to go along with the ride with a grateful and joyous heart, or we can choose to struggle against it only to end up miserable and hurt.

The essence of the first discipline is this: take responsibility and control over your desires, thoughts, actions, and what is in your control, and leave the rest to providence or the cosmos. Learn to live your life in the present, the only thing in our control and the only place and time where life happens. Learn to accept and appreciate your circumstances—even the bad ones—for they are unique to you and meant to prepare you for the life nature intends for you—*living in accordance with nature.*

Action: The Second Discipline

"Say to yourself at the start of the day, I shall meet with meddling, ungrateful, violent, treacherous, envious, and unsociable people. They are subject to all these defects because they have no knowledge of good and bad. But I, who have observed the nature of the good, and seen that it is the right; and of the bad, and seen that it is the wrong; and of the wrongdoer himself, and seen that his nature is akin to my own—not because he is of the same blood and seed, but because he shares as I do in mind and thus in a portion of the divine—I, then, can neither be harmed by these people, nor become angry with one who is akin to me, nor can I hate him, for we have come into being to work together, like feet, hands, eyelids, or the two rows of teeth in our upper and lower jaws. To work against one another is therefore contrary to nature; and to be angry with another person and turn away from him is surely to work against him."

Marcus Aurelius, Meditations 2.1

The discipline of action, or the impulse to action, is the practical application of the three stoic topos of ethics in our daily lives.

This discipline concerns itself with the tenet of ethics that concentrates on what stoicism considers good, bad, and indifferent. Because the topos of ethics also relates to how to live a good, happy, or fulfilled life, the aim of the practical application of this discipline is to lead to a eudemonic life, a life governed by the virtues of self-discipline, self-control, courage, justice, and wisdom.

Here, what you ought to keep in mind that the underlying principle behind stoicism is that virtue is the only true good and therefore, its practice alone is enough to help you live a good, fulfilling life.

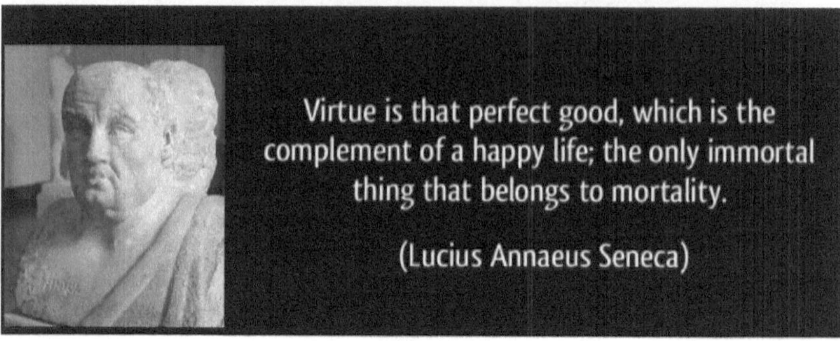

The discipline of action is about living in harmony with nature and all living things including the people in your social circle as well as humankind in general. This means accepting providence and wishing ill will on no one but wishing that all humankind should flourish and prosper in all undertakings and achieve happiness as the ultimate goal of life.

However, as a stoic, you must recognize that making other people happy or fostering someone's wellbeing is outside your immediate control; the only thing any of us can do is wish others well, act with virtue towards others, and adopt an accepting and detached approach towards what comes of our actions. Principally, this means to practice the discipline of action, you need to act in accordance with rational appraisal of desired outcome but at the same time practice acceptance and detachment from the outcome—success or failure.

When your desires lead to action in the present moment, the only moment we have and where life happens, question whether, *(1)* you have undertaken it "with a reserve clause,"

(2) your actions are complimentary to the overall good or serving a common welfare," and *(3)* that the action is valuable.

The discipline of action is, according to Hadot, a thought leader in stoic studies, "action that serves mankind" and for good reason. This discipline calls on you to practice oikeiosis, to widen your circle of self-love, and treat other human beings with the same care and affection you would offer yourself as well as to do what you can do to foster the physical and mental wellbeing and happiness of all humankind. Early stoics called this process "stoic philanthropy" or "love of mankind."

STOIC LOVE

- As others are external to us, though, we can only "prefer" that they flourish, while accepting their imperfection, folly, and vice, as inevitable and beyond our direct control – with the Stoic "reserve clause", in other words.

- We should not discriminate between others, but should aspire to expand our sense of natural affection to encompass the rest of humanity, an attitude sometimes called Stoic "philanthropy" or love of mankind.

- The Sage is not obsessed with anyone, in part, because he loves everyone as much as he is able

Lived Ethics: How to Apply the Discipline of Action

The underlying teaching behind this discipline is that of developing your love for others so that your behaviors—towards others—are congruent with the virtue of justice and ethics in general. Remember the stoic teaching: "virtue is the only good." When you live a life governed by virtue, your life will be in accordance with nature and therefore, you are likely to experience happiness in your life. As Marcus Aurelius noted in The Meditations:

"Men exist for the sake of one another. Teach them then or bear with them."

Marcus Aurelius, Meditations

Essentially, ancient stoics taught that because it is in our control, we should aim to love others, even those who are hateful to us. As Aurelius notes, at the start of the day, we should acknowledge that throughout our day, we will meet people who are envious, unsociable, and even violent; our aim, then, should be to, because we are all connected by logos, universal reason, and are part of the same cosmos, approach them with a glad heart and wish them well.

Worth noting and mentioning is that stoicism is an action-based philosophy that calls on you to practice the three disciplines as the ultimate path to prokopton, making progress. Because of their interdependence, you cannot practice any of the disciplines in isolation. To practice the discipline of action, you must also practice the discipline of desire and assent.

Assent: The Third Discipline

Synkatathesis-Assent

- *Synkatathesis*-3rd faculty of the human soul, the power of giving or withholding assent to representations

- The Stoics intuition that assent is an essential faculty of the human soul draws attention to their interest in the self, the first-person perspective, what each individual does with his experience. Any representation is a part of my experience, but I can make it *mine,*- my outlook, or belied, or commitment- or *not mine,* by giving or withholding assent (Long 274).

- Giving assent to a representation allows for action

Regarded as stoic mindfulness, the discipline of assent (synkatathesis) relates to the practical application of the stoic topos of logic. The primary aim of this discipline is to teach you how to live in harmony with human nature guided by the principles of reason and truthfulness of thought and speech.

This discipline is more than truthfulness or wisdom. It is about developing the ability to be continually aware of our inner self, our judgments, beliefs, and their residual actions especially keeping in mind how these relate to our ability to live free, virtuously, and in accordance with nature.

As used by early stoics, the term "judgement" is generalist in nature. In relation to this, being a sage is about developing the ability to monitor and evaluate your judgment and beliefs and determine if they are complementary to the practice of the cardinal virtues whose adherence to leads to happiness or well-being. This is of utmost important.

Stoicism recognizes that our thoughts, emotions, desires, and actions are the fruits of our judgement. When our judgments are not virtue-based or in tune with nature or the cosmos, the results are the irrational vices and passions that sages ought to be indifferent to or seek to overcome.

By being openly mindful and aware of your thoughts, beliefs, and judgments, you can notice the early signs of irrational, unhealthy, or upsetting thoughts, judgements or impressions and by becoming aware, teach yourself how to take a step back and question them or as stoicism states, "withhold assent or agreement with them."

The practical implications of this is that by practicing the discipline of assent, it becomes easier to notice emotion, thoughts, beliefs, and judgments—especially ones that appear negative or unwanted—and to take a step back instead of agreeing with these sentiments and allowing them to carry you away into irrational judgments and unhealthy vices and passions.

The third stoic principle calls for prosochê, the ability to become attentive to your conscious mind as it uses logic to draw conclusions that lead to actions. We call this discipline stoic mindfulness because becoming attentive of the judgements of your conscious mind requires moment-to-moment awareness, the ability to reside in the present.

In addition, this discipline is about being able to control our emotions and using our conscious, decision-making abilities, decided what about our present reality we accept or do not accept–the very definition of making judgment or logic-based decisions. The chapter that follows discusses the stoic way to handle emotions.

Lived Logic: How to Practice the Discipline of Assent

The assent process, i.e. assenting to a judgement or agreeing to a perception, has four main stages. (1) ***Perception***, how we perceive an external circumstance or event; (2) ***Judgment***, out of our perception, we draw a seemingly unconscious or involuntary judgment; (3) ***Proposition***, our perception forms an impression and presents it to our conscious reasoning/logic, and (4) ***assent,*** we agree or reject the proposition or withhold judgment.

Practical application of the discipline of assent in your daily life as a sage calls on you to protect yourself, the discerning self, from incorrect judgments. The best way to do this is to teach your conscious mind how to be a good judge of judgments and perceptions especially ones enforced on you by daily circumstances, your social circle, and other external elements such as the media and events not within your control. Keep in mind what Epictetus said about assenting to wrong impressions: it leads to unhappiness:

In addition to the above, as a sage, you should also question your irrational thoughts and judgments. You can do this by asking yourself self-reflecting questions such as "why am I feeling this way?" "What do I dislike about this situation?" "What about this irritates or irks me and why?"

Asking yourself self-reflecting questions allows you to question your judgments and do what stoics call "cleaning your inner citadel," the inner self (or "I") that acts as our guiding principle. To nurture the habit of questioning your presuppositions, teach yourself how to cultivate attentiveness (or mindfulness) of the present moment, the existing events, people, and things. From this, you can teach your consciousness how to question the nature and value of emotional sentiments or reactions.

Another suggestion comes from Marcus Aurelius; he notes that to practice the discipline of assent, you should circumscribe yourself.

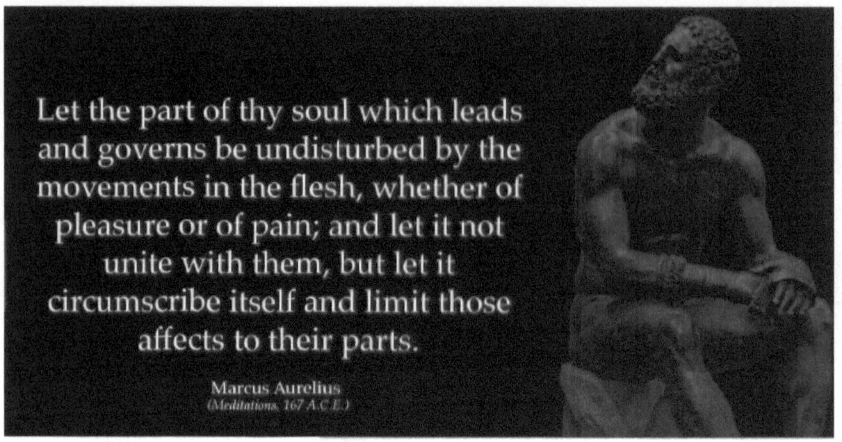

According to the teachings of Marcus Aurelius in The Meditations, circumscribing the self is narrowing our attention and focus to the present moment and on our impulses, perceptions, and actions in the NOW.

This is especially important because being a sage is about realizing that life happens in the present moment, and because you have complete control over your present, you should be indifferent to the past and the future (and its many desires).

How do you circumscribe yourself? *Meditations* 12.3, offers invaluable insight.

12.3   There are three things of which you are composed: body, breath, and mind.* Of these, the first two are your own in so far as it is your duty to take care of them; but only the third is your own in the full sense. So if you will put away from yourself – that is to say, from your mind – all that others do or say, and all that you yourself have done or said, and all that troubles you with regard to the future, and all that belonging to the body which envelops you and the breath conjoined with it is attached to you independently of your will, and all that the vortex whirling around outside you sweeps in its wake, so that the power of your mind, thus delivered from the bonds of fate, may live a pure and unfettered life alone with itself, doing what is just, desiring what comes to pass, and saying what is true – if, I say, you will put away from your governing faculty all that accretes to it from the affections of the body, and all that lies in the future or in time gone by, and make yourself, in Empedocles' words, 'a well-rounded sphere rejoicing in the solitude around it', and strive to live only the life that is your own, that is to say, your present life, then you will be able to pass at least the time that is left to you until you die in calm and kindliness, and as one who is at peace with the guardian-spirit that dwells within him.

According to this teaching, three elements, body, breath, and mind, form our true nature. Of these, although your body and breath are under your care, they are outside your immediate control; the mind, on the other hand, you have complete control over.

To circumscribe yourself, therefore, you have to become continuously aware of the things outside your control. You have no control over the past, the future, other people, destiny, and unconscious emotions; thus, your perception towards these things should be that they should have no influence on your judgment (self) in the present moment.

Realizing and accepting this reality allows you to experience inner serenity; with serenity comes an inner state of happiness that is not reliant on external circumstances. In fact, once you realize that you are capable of controlling your mind and guarding its "state" against the difficulties/vicissitudes of life, the idea of living a virtuous, eudemonic life becomes easier to grasp and emulate in your day-to-day, moment-to-moment existence.

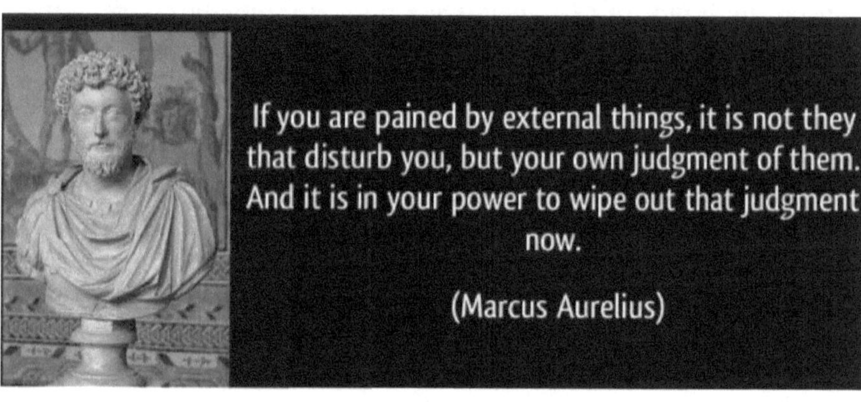

To practice the discipline of assent, embrace the principle of prokoton, making progress, as an integral part of your life. This starts with implementing the basic stoic tenet of informal logic for as Epictetus noted:

"That is why, I suppose, the philosophers put logic first, just as, when it comes to measuring grain, we begin by examining the measure. For, unless we first determine what a bushel and what a balance is, how shall we be able to measure or weigh anything?"

Epictetus, Discourses 1.17.6-7

Since stoicism is holistic and interconnected, practicing the topos of logic without practicing other two topois will fail to yield the results you desire in your life. That noted—that you should practice all the topois and disciplines together because stoicism is holistic—the underlying principle behind the discipline of assent is to cultivate the ability to attention to how you perceive and judge external circumstances or events.

To do this, you need to become aware or mindful and practice detachment from surrounding circumstance because after all, the only thing you have complete control over is your inner state. Embody what stoicism notes: *"it is not circumstances that cause you emotional anguish but your thoughts and perceptions of those circumstances or events."* Since your thoughts, perception, and judgments are the only things within your complete control, choose to direct them towards living a life of virtue, which inadvertently, will influence the future you create for yourself and others as well.

Here is Marcus Aurelius on how to practice the discipline of assent:

"Venerate your faculty of judgement. For it depends entirely on this that there should never arise in your ruling centre any judgement that fails to accord with nature or with the constitution of a rational being; and it is this that guarantees freedom from hasty judgement, and fellowship with humankind, and obedience to the gods."

Marcus Aurelius, Meditations 3.9

As illustrated here, like the three topois, the three disciplines have great overlaps. Implementing them together will allow you to make progress towards living a life that is in accordance with nature—human and cosmic nature.

In the next chapter, we look at how to use stoic principles to become emotionally strong and resilient:

Chapter 6: The Stoic Path to Emotional Resiliency, Confidence, & Wisdom

To create a eudemonic life, stoicism holds that we must practice apatheia. Epictetus defined apatheia as "freedom from passion, a constituent of the *eudaimôn* life."

In stoicism, passion does not mean emotion. The aim of being a stoic is not to live a passionless life or to suppress your emotions. On the contrary, the aim of apatheia (and the stoic philosophy in general) is to help you differentiate between healthy and unhealthy passions, the latter of which includes passions such as pleasure, pain, craving, and fear and the former of which includes delight, willing, and discretion. Except for pain, most of these "passions" are opposites:

In stoicism, passions are not unconscious or automatic, and because of this, their experience is entirely in our control because they result from our judgments and assent to specific "external or internal" circumstances.

To this end, it is worth noting that when sages refer to the passion of "fear," they are not referring to it in the sense of our innate automatic response to fearful stimuli (the fight-or-flight response); they are referring to the perception that forms after you start considering the causative factors.

When it comes to handling emotions, becoming emotionally strong and resilient, stoicism teaches that some responses are automatic and therefore outside our control. Our focus, therefore, should not be on such responses. Emotional strength and resiliency comes from being aware of what is in your control in any circumstance and then making the deliberate choice to focus on that.

How stoicism approaches emotions or "passions" is very similar to how neuroscience and cognitive behavioral therapy (CBT) approach emotions. Like stoicism, neuroscience recognizes that fear is an unconscious and automatic response that forms as a defense mechanism. Like psychology—CBT is a psychological approach—stoicism also recognizes the complexity of emotions. In the case of fear, it (stoicism) notes that while it is a defense mechanism, it also has a conscious aspect where the mind—the rational self— uses the fear stimuli to create a perception based on memories, logic, upbringing, etc.

Using the example of dealing with pain, the stoic philosophy recognizes that pain is more than the sensation; it is also the desire to avoid things, events, and circumstances we adjudge as bad or unwanted.

Now that we are living in relatively safe spaces where we do not have to run away from or fight off saber-toothed cats or crocodilians, the fight-or-flight response has become largely redundant.

In the modern world, when we experience fear, it is not because we are in danger, it is because we are irrationally anticipating or expecting the happenstance of something we consider "bad" or unwanted—psychology calls this catastrophizing or playing out what-if situations.

When you are craving something, you are irrationally striving to attain or achieve something you have mistakenly concluded is good or desired. Pleasure, on its part, is an irrational euphoria over something you consider "good or pleasurable" but that under scrutiny proves unworthy of choosing.

To practice emotional resiliency, stoicism suggests that we concentrate on the *eupatheiai,* the healthy passions. This ability comes from awareness and the continued desire (and resolution) to avoid harmful things and vices—those that are not complimentary to living a virtuous life.

Underpinning your ability to develop emotional resiliency is this one thing: to practice level-headedness—sages call it equanimity—in the face of challenges/difficulties that life throws at you, which will be many.

*Our thoughts drive our reality.

*We are disturbed not by what happens to us but by our thoughts about what happens.

*If our thoughts are filled with stress, we subject our bodies to inflammation—the proven root of nearly all illness.

*Thoughts are not facts.

Emotional intelligence and resiliency develops out of an ability to be logical and to apply reason to whatever circumstance or experience. When you start doing this, you learn how to overlook things that lack meaning and to focus on the things that matter the most to you.

In addition to what we have discussed, to use stoicism or stoic principles to develop emotional strength and resiliency, implement the following strategies to your daily circumstances:

1: Contemplate the worst-case scenario

In Meditations, Marcus Aurelius writes:

Given that Aurelius is the stoic philosopher known to most of us, why would he advise us to imagine a situation where the people we meet during the day shall be insolent, selfish, and disloyal? Is being an enthusiast, to expect the best, not better, after all, does the law of attraction not state that we attract into our lives what we think?

The teaching behind this advice is to accustom your mind to, or rather, to prepare it for any eventuality so that when bad things happen, they will not affect your perception in the same way that they would had you not anticipated it.

Take the example of anticipating meeting "difficult" people. By anticipating it, you will come to the realization that you cannot control what others say or do. There is a difference between being a pessimist and reminding yourself that the worse can happen.

Early stoics were in the habit of contemplating their demise; they would spend a few minutes of their day thinking about the worst that could happen, including their death, a practice called *memento mori*, then they would let the thoughts just pass and refocus their consciousness on experiencing life in the present moment.

> *"Let us prepare our minds as if we'd come to the very end of life. Let us postpone nothing. Let us balance life's books each day. ... The one who puts the finishing touches on their life each day is never short of time."*
> *Seneca*

Contemplating events—especially ones you perceive as bad or unwanted—in advance is an invaluable strategy that helps you realign your expectations; when your expectations are in control, or at the very least, hinged on a reality of what may happen, you are less likely to feel frustrated when the unexpected happens.

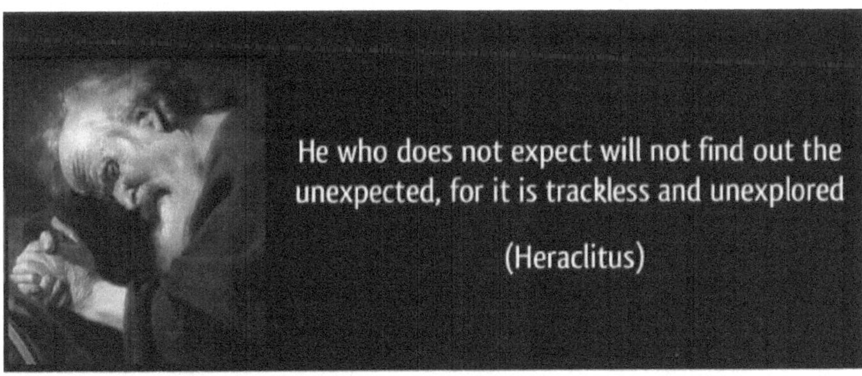

Seneca points out that "projecting your thoughts before you," which you do by imagining all conceivable scenarios, makes you mentally strong enough to cope with any eventuality that may occur. Is this not what we now refer to as emotional or mental resiliency?

2: Practice hupexhairesis

Hupexhairesis is a stoic term coined by Epictetus; it means using a reverse clause. Many are the times when you have used terms such as "God willing" or "If fate allows." Usage of such terms shows your awareness of part of the outcome being outside your control.

By becoming aware of this fact, you open yourself to the possibility of things not working out as you may want or intend, the effect of which is that when the unexpected becomes reality, it does not throw your self-esteem through the wringer.

Mind you, acknowledging that you are not 100% in control of the outcome—and are therefore not 100% responsible for it— is not a license to be undisciplined or lazy. The awareness here is that you are only in control of your actions, the process, but never the outcome.

Applying the reverse clause in all your life circumstances allows you to focus on what you do control, which is your "self." Thinking you have control over outcomes is a cause of pain, frustration, and a host of other unhealthy emotions whose impact on your wellbeing and happiness is negative.

When you concentrate on the process, your actions, and do all you can, fate or God permitting, things usually turn out well. As Seneca so elegantly articulated it:

"In short, the wise man looks to the purpose of all actions, not their consequences; beginnings are in our power but Fortune judges the outcome, and I do not grant her verdict upon me."

Seneca

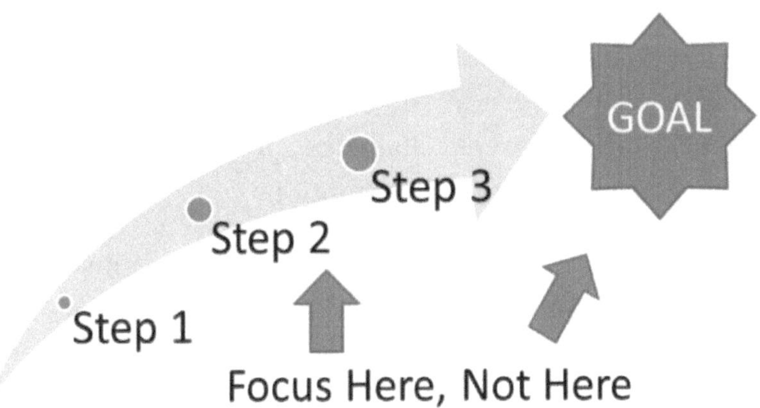

3: Change your perspective

There is no doubt that life's many situations and challenges will get you down and beat you to a point of breaking you. It is normal to feel bad about failing to achieve the expected, to feel beaten and defeated. What is normal is allowing your defeat to become your new circumstance.

If there is one stoic teaching that will teach you how to be emotionally stronger, wiser, more confident, and successful, it is that whenever you are feeling bad, whenever things fail to pan out as expected, instead of giving up, viewing the defeat as a permanent pronouncement, the sage change his perspective.

Remember this: what you focus on becomes your perception. If you focus on how emotionally awful you feel, how defeated you are, how unconfident you feel, these are the realities you will notice in your life, and thus, you will attract circumstances that reinforce these realities.

When a challenge or setback leaves you feeling emotionally distraught, your view of the world narrows. Instead of seeing your life as a long journey, you start seeing your entire life as dictated by the present challenge or setback, a perfect breeding ground for unhealthy emotions.

Like most of us, a sage experiences challenges and setbacks. However, unlike most of us, when this happens, a sage takes a step back and works to gain perspective.

Seneca pointed out:

"A man is as miserable as he thinks he is."

Seneca

Marcus Aurelius added to this by saying:

Stoicism teaches that to overcome challenges and setbacks, which is how you develop confidence, wisdom, and emotional resiliency, you should adopt a "view from above." This means adopting a cosmic view, seeing yourself from a bird's eye view. When you do this, you gain perspective.

Compared to the area in which you live, your city, your country, your continent, the world, the Milky Way, the universe, etc., your problems, challenges, or setbacks become small and even inconsequential.

The essence of this practice is not to belittle yourself or show you how insignificant you are, no. The essence of the practice is to show you the narrowness of your perception. In the grand scheme of things, your challenges, problems, and setbacks are small.

Failing is not the end of the world. You have screwed up many times before and your world did not shutter. Changing your perspective allows you to avoid focusing illusion, blowing things out of proportion, a great example of which is thinking that failing or screwing up is the start of the end of your world.

4: Think "what would a sage do?"

"Contemplation of the sage" is one of the most important stoic rituals. The underlying teaching here is that whenever you are feeling low in confidence, emotionally drained, or you would like some practical wisdom, find a role model, someone that can inspire you (a sage), and that you can look up to and emulate.

Thinking about a role model, someone you would like to emulate, can give you the strength, guidance, resilience, and fortitude you need to keep focus on what you can control and how to keep moving forward.

This is what Seneca meant when he stated:

"Choose someone whose way of life as well as words, and whose very face as mirroring the character that lies behind it, have won your approval. Be always pointing him out to yourself either as your guardian or as your model. There is a need, in my view, for someone as a standard against which our characters can measure themselves. Without a ruler to do it against you won't make crooked straight."

Thinking about someone you admire, someone that models the virtues and character traits you would like to make part of your "self," is a scientifically proven way to improve your confidence, emotional resiliency, and decision making skills.

If you want to become more confident, picture someone who is confident, and the next time you need to be confident, ask yourself, "what would X do if he/she were in a similar situation?" If the goal is to become wiser, the next time you are about to make an important decision, have in mind someone you consider wise, and then ask yourself what he or she would do. Apply the same principle to being resilient and emotionally strong.

5: Practice acknowledgment

A sage acknowledges that emotions or passions are internal, developed by perceptions of the "self." Marcus Aurelius noted:

"Today I escaped anxiety. Or no, I discarded it, because it was within me, in my own perceptions — not outside." — Marcus Aurelius, Meditations

Whatever you feel, be it pain, pleasure, delight, or any other form of emotion or experience, is partly external and largely externally-driven. Whatever you tell yourself about your life experience and the events that make up your daily life is more important than what happens to you. Our perceptions create our judgments and feelings. Because our perception is in our control, we should be mindful of what we give life to.

Become aware of, and acknowledge the fact that nothing—or no one—can hurt you, demoralize you, or break you unless you view it as such and give it power. Whenever you are facing a challenge, a failure, or obstacle, look within, acknowledge, and then question the story you are telling yourself. If the stories the "self" is narrating are not complementary to the practice of virtue, change your perception as illustrated in the previous strategy.

6: Practice misfortune

This stoic practice is very similar to contemplating the worst-case scenario but different in the sense that here, in the words of Seneca:

"It is in times of security that the spirit should be preparing itself for difficult times; while fortune is bestowing favors on it is then is the time for it to be strengthened against her rebuffs."

Seneca

How do you practice misfortune and how does it make you resilient, confident, and wise?

First, worth noting is that Seneca was wealthy; he was an advisor to Nero the tyrannical emperor. Even though he was wealthy, he would set aside a number of days each month where he would practice poverty, living as if he had nothing. He ate little food, wore the worst clothes, and slept as if he were poor, away from the comfort of his warm home and bed. He did this because he wanted to prepare himself for any eventuality and most importantly, to face the things he feared.

Likewise, we should strive to get outside our comfort zones, to face the things or circumstance we fear and like Seneca, ask, "Is this what I so feared?"

Fear and anxiety are the main causes of unhealthy emotions. When you make a deliberate effort to come face to face with the very thing you fear, you deny it power over your inner self, and as you know when you become aware of the reality that you are in control of your perception and thoughts, your approach towards life and its many circumstances changes.

Conclusion

Thank you for reading this guide.

I trust that you found it immensely educational and profoundly actionable.

As you probably noted, while stoicism is an age-old philosophy, its tenets, principles and practices are still as actionable as ever. If you implement the various strategies and practices we have discussed throughout this guide, you will become resilient, emotionally strong, confident, and wise.

Importantly, stoicism is a practical philosophy. From what you have learned in this guide, implement what seems most practical to you. Remember the stoic teaching of *prokopê*, making progress, and make it part of your daily existence.

Do You Like My Book & Approach To Publishing?

If you like my writing and style and would love the ease of learning literally everything you can get your hands on from Fantonpublishers.com, I'd really need you to do me either of the following favors.

1: First, I'd Love It If You Leave a Review of This Book on Amazon.

2: Do You Want More Books?

To get a list of all my other books, please visit fantonpublishers.com, my author central or let me send you the list by requesting them below: http://bit.ly/2fantonpubnewbooks

3: Grab Some Freebies On Your Way Out; Giving Is Receiving, Right?

I gave you a complimentary book at the start of the book. If you are still interested, grab it here.

5 Pillar Life Transformation Checklist: http://bit.ly/2fantonfreebie